SUP

To

Gerry,

Hope you enjoy

it,

Ellie xx

WAKE

Poetry & Short Stories

by Ellie Rose McKee

Written by Ellie Rose McKee
www.ellierose101.co.uk

Cover Photo Location: Northern Ireland's North Coast (near The Giant's Causeway)

Published by Lulu
ISBN: 978-1-291-09868-6

About the Author

Ellie was born and raised in Northern Ireland and has lived in England on and off since; spending three years in Lincoln, where she went to university, and six months in Oxford. She enjoys travelling, photography, making YouTube videos and eating chocolate cake.

When not writing, Ellie invests her time in children's and youth work as well as a wide variety of volunteer work.

Also by Ellie Rose McKee

- Still Dreaming: Poetry & Short Stories

- Overlooked Awe (Photobook)

- Creature's Comfort (Photobook – Coming Soon)

- Rising from Ashes (Novel – Coming Soon)

Dedicated to my 14 year old self
I may be someone different now, but I'll never forget you.

"Here comes the rain again
falling from the stars
drenched in my pain again
becoming who we are

As my memory rests
but never forgets what I lost
Wake me up when September ends."

- *Green Day*

Contents

Introduction

This book is the sequel to 'Still Dreaming' and, as I said in SD's preface, the double sided imagery in the titles of these books is intended. Both books speak of, among other things, sleep and death. Still Dreaming focused more on sleep, however, and WAKE focuses more on death. Not just death of people, though; death of things, such as relationships and ways of life.

Fret not, dear reader; this book is not completely negative despite discussing some difficult topics. Death of some things can be good, after all. It can be just what is needed before the birth of new, better things.

I dedicated this book to my younger self because it seemed like an obvious thing to do. If I had read these words back then, specifically the words of the poems 'Note to Self' and 'Triumph', it would have really helped. Aside from that, though, it must be noted that the person I once was, and what that person went through, helped shape many of the stories listed here.

Speaking of the symbolism behind WAKE's inscription – there's a reason why I released this book when I did; I'll let you figure out what that means by yourself, but I will say this: It is true that both in pain and in the battle of coming through it, we become who we are; more than we would have, if all we'd ever known was an easy life.

During my teenage years I wrote approximately fifty poems, each more horribly depressing than the last. Looking back, I must admit, a lot of it makes me cringe but there were a few verses, however, that stuck out to me as either well written or worth saying and these segments have been pieced together to form 'AGNST' as it appears in this book. I would like to state one last time: I'm not the little girl that penned those words anymore and I don't look at life in quite the same way. I now have answers to all the questions posed within the text, but still think they're good questions to ask.

I suppose there's irony in the fact that one of the first stories in this collection is about an ending. This was not intentional but I suppose it just goes to emphasise what I was saying about endings needing to come before new things can truly start.

Yet another parallel between Still Dreaming and WAKE is this – both 'The Coffeehouse' (short story in S.D.) and 'The Dance Floor' (monologue included here, in WAKE) were inspired by people watching.
I set out purposefully, to gain inspiration for a story, in the first instance but not in the second and, as such, it wasn't a parallel I noticed right away.
I say in 'The Dance Floor' that I wrote it in my head while on a night out, memorized it and wrote it down on paper at a later date – this is indeed true.

The sonnet, 'Three Huge Words', talks about words that are not large in term of size or numbers of letters, but massive in terms of meaning; hence the use of the term 'small-huge' in the third stanza.

I believe the following fact to be obvious, but I state it just in case it is not: The person the poem 'Three Huge Words' is directed at and the person the poem 'Now That We're Done' is directed at are not one and the same – far from it. If the people concerned ever read said poems, which they probably never will, then they will know it is about them without me ever having to say.

I suppose you could say 'Daydreaming' and 'Time' are parodies of each other; viewing the same things from different perspectives. You may also find it interesting to note that they are either side of a story that deals with the grief.

'Born of Death', in a much earlier form that is very unlike what you see before you here, was originally written as an entry for the Bridport Prize Short Story competition circa 2006 and 'Away with the Fairies' is, as you may have guessed, an exaggerated parody of elements within my own personality.

The short story ‘The Room at the End of the Hall’ displays what lives overlapping due to time not being linear (a concept touched upon in ‘Time’) might look like if it were to play out in a more obvious way.

‘Note to Self’ was partly inspired by Mother Teresa’s Poem ‘Anyway’.

I tried out a greater variety of literary styles here, than I had previously experimented with elsewhere, mainly to challenge myself as a writer.

I hope you like it.

P.S. If you can find the Doctor Who reference among these pages, you get ultimate brownie points.

Instructions for Reading

I request that you still yourself,

For just a moment or two.

Breathe deeply,

Clear your mind.

Sit down,

Take time.

Read slowly and,

Ponder a while.

Savour the sentiments,

And, above all else,

Enjoy.

A Stormy Ending

Janet had once heard divorce described as an emotional storm, but she had never thought she would ever experience it for herself.

“It’s not your fault; I don’t want you blaming yourself. Sometimes these things just happen” said Mom - as much to herself as to Janet.

“It being my fault hadn’t even crossed my mind” she replied, adding “but it’s firmly in there now” quietly, to herself.

“How could I have been so oblivious to this?” Janet questioned, with fresh tears forming in her eyes.

“I guess I hid it well. My teachers always said I had an acting talent… I wanted to be an actress y’know. But all that ended when, well, when I married your dad”.

Janet sighed. “So it wasn’t just my dreams he enjoyed crushing then”.

“Afraid not”.

Leaning in to give her mother a reassuring rub of the shoulder, Janet pulled back sharply at the fresh wave of agony, smeared across her mother's face.

"I'm sorry, I'm sorry" Janet pleaded "I wasn't thinking!"

"It's okay, it's okay" said Janet's mom, through gritted teeth. "It didn't hurt that much, really". She was now white with pain.

"I'll try phoning the ambulance again; I don't know what's keeping them".

As Janet reached for the phone once more, her father re-entered the room.

"That won't be necessary" he said, in a hard, emotionless tone.

Domestic violence was another storm Janet never thought she'd have to go through.

AGNST

I

Another paradox, what a surprise

Life is not easy

Open your eyes

Stop faking joy, for joy's own sake

To live a lie is your mistake!

Trying to be a better person

To escape my faults and fears

As many others have tried,

Right down through the years

II

Wounds from life and wounds from love

Could it all be controlled from above?

Can we leave our lives to fate -

When all we do is obliterate?

People of the past were no better

People of the future will be no worse

The grass is NOT greener on the other side

Is it that we're colour-blind?

Rose tinted spectacles, fooling the mind

III

I can't win and you won't lose

Both too stubborn to give up and refuse

Stupid cycles that have gone on years

Only ever getting worse and resulting in tears

I tried quitting, tried to go my own way

Never thought I'd end up back here, in the same place one day

It's awful and traumatic; I really can't stand it

There have been too many fights between these four walls

Crashing, screaming – the full show

Never learning to let things go

Always holding grudges, repeating past mistakes

Reopening old wounds

IV

There are things I've never told you

And probably never will

There are feelings that I've locked inside

So deep they've made me ill

They've became a part of me

In a sick and twisted way

But I don't want you to feel the guilt

So they are words that I'll never say

V

Scared of nothing

For my fears ARE nothing – meaningless

Today, tomorrow

The days all seem to bleed

Is anything significant?

I can't go back now

'Cause this is how I feel

Living in this turmoil

How can this be real?

It may seem like one endless torture to some

But look back and see how far we've come

We've battled it and will again

So does this ever really end?

VI

Everything is complicated

Everything is hard

We're screwed if this is held against us

But the joy's in taking part

(Right?)

Will I always feel this way?

Will my pain depart?

What are the secrets that unlock this beating heart?

I pray the taunts never last

That they would stay forever past

VII

Irrational my thought

Yet somehow clear to me

How do I discover, who I'm meant to be?

All my life, I just wait

Nothing to anticipate

Just waiting

For a purpose, I suppose

My soul is trapped and my body tired

Waiting until I have expired

Us to dust and dust to ash

What will happen when our feelings truly clash?

Ambition is a deadly trait

And ignorance has no fear

I don't know how I'll cope

I've I'm stuck here, like this, one more year

VIII

Finished for now or for forever

To find the key I must endeavour

For what's the use in idol thought

- if no action is therefore brought?

I have given in to giving up

But will soon start to rebuild

Begin again

- a fresh start, in a life without pain

The Dance Floor

The music is blaring and, although it's not my kind of song, I hold firm to my opinion that almost everything sounds better when turned as loud as it can go.

Kev's leaning in, towards my ear, to ask me why I'm not dancing. I point towards my empty glass and head toward the bar where I'll refill my drink.

I don't want to dance and previous experience has thought me I can get away with standing on the sidelines for quite long periods of time before someone notices, as Kev just did.

Of course I love to dance, just not in front of other people.

Happy to gently sway from side to side along with the beat though; swaying seems to be socially acceptable enough.

The barman is taking an age to acknowledge my presence, which is fine seeing as I'm not in a hurry. The people either side of me, however, seem to be quite agitated by his speed (or lack thereof). They are served first.

Do not misunderstand me; I am enjoying myself – in my own little way.
I don't feel the need to enjoy myself in anyone else's way.

I survey the dance floor. It is filled. People are everywhere. As I notice some girls I went to high school with a few tables over I avert my eyes and turn back round towards the bar. Mr barman is waiting impatiently for my order.
"Diet coke" I say.
"What?" he says.
"Diet coke".
"Coke?"
"Yes. Diet."
He hands me a regular coke and I pay before returning to my corner, beside the speaker, where I will sip it slowly. I would be irritated by the barman's inability to hear me if I wasn't so deaf myself.
I *am* irritated by how much I paid for something that wasn't quite what I wanted, however.

A song I like eventually comes on and I see my brother swaying in the opposite corner of the club. Not quite as sober as I.

After spilling most of what must be his 4th drink since arriving here he sets it down and immediately forgets where. Looking around, he spots the barman and goes to buy two more drinks – both for himself, one for each hand. Again, he spills more of these than he drinks.

He had been drinking with the others, before getting as far as the club. I had a couple of 'alcopops' at that time myself, but they were too fizzy for my liking. I am a whiskey girl after all.

Yes, I'm a fan of Mr Jack Daniels' fine beverages. My wallet, though, is not; so, I suppose it's a good thing I'm not in the mood to consume *real* drinks this eve

Out of sheer luck, another song I like comes on, but it reminds me of someone whom I do not wish to be reminded of.

I take out my phone, about to text said person but relent almost immediately.

Kev is dancing with someone I vaguely recognise; seems to be really enjoying himself.
It strikes me that, while I am not fond of the regular – crowded coffee shop kind, I really enjoy this sort of people watching. It fascinates me in an odd way; for reasons I don't fully understand.

My sister and her friend alike are dancing like joyous wild things; revelling in their youth. It makes me smile but the smile is taken away by the person who just bumped into me and sprayed my feet with alcohol. I sigh and make a mental note to clean my shoes the minute I get home.

I go to the toilets not because I need to use them but because I want a brief break from swaying.
In the cubical I throw my hands up and dance, because no one can see me.

After a moment or two I stop and consider my social awkwardness with contempt. "Why can't I dance in front of other people?" I ask myself, inwardly.

Upon returning to the edge of the dance floor, I see my brother is doing a circuit of it. He stumbles for a few yards then stops, as if contemplating life, he looks around, sways a bit to the music and then moves a few more yards. By this point he has a full glass of water in one hand and a full beer in the other, having not touched either since their purchase some fifteen minutes prior.

My sister has stopped dancing now, she's sitting with her friend – both engrossed in whatever is on their respective phone's awfully bright screens.

The desire to text a certain person wells up again but I ignore it and send out a tweet containing song lyrics instead. Miracle upon miracle – the club has now played three songs that fit my taste.

My taste in music is not in the least bit limited, yet most venues of this variety somehow manage to navigate my eclectic preferences, without touching upon them, quite well.

Just before I return my phone to my pocket I glance at the time, suspecting the place will be closing soon.

I am right.

Kev, my brother, sister and her friend have congregated and given each other the nod, implying they will leave now.

I follow without being acknowledged in the nodding agreement, as always.

We step out into the cold night and get a face full of second hand smoke. Each other member of my group curls up their noses, while I breathe in as much as I can get away with – without choking or making it obvious.

In that moment I wished I had a cigarette of my own.

I do enjoy them, I cannot lie, but I've never been addicted and to take them in moderation is apparently looked down upon more so than using them a lot.

I've been told before that I both no not smoke and no not enjoy it, because I only ever put a little white stick to my mouth every few months or so.
Oh how I hate it when people tell me what I like, or what I do. These people do not know me, but, I digress. Temptation has a way of capturing your mind and taking it away, but I have regained my thought. Just in time to see the people I'm going home with spilt in two very different directions.

My sister and Kev head towards the queue of people, waiting to be picked up. While my brother and my sister's friend go towards the source of late night nourishment. If you could class burgers and overcooked pizza as nourishment, that is.

A man just punched another of his kind and it didn't take the police long to jump on both of them.
I shudder, reminded of how much witnessing violence traumatises my soul.

Having followed my sister and Kev, I stand and shiver at the back of the queue. Soon my brother returns only to saunter off again, a moment later. Kev and my sister's friend decide to walk home just as the rain starts to drip from above.

My sister and I wait for quite some time before a cab becomes available. Just in time, my brother returns and takes his place in the front passenger seat. There is no conversation between the three of us and the driver other than stating our intended destination and confirming the fare.

They say artists and writers alike find inspiration in the oddest of placesand I don't know if you consider the dance floor to be an odd place, dear reader, but I certainly do.

All of these words, now in front of you, I am writing in my head. As I have stood and watched tonight pass by I planned each paragraph.

I memorized each one and rehearsed them in the taxi home.

My sister and Kev gained memories from the night out, as well as a few Facebook photos. My brother a headache I'm quite sure, but I take away with me this short story – of sorts.

Just another night out.

Three Huge Words

'Twas the darkest time of my life, to date
And you were there, listening, despite it all
I am glad you stuck around, at any rate
The 'reasons to leave' list was so very tall

I still appreciate the help, even now
Now I'm through it and you are not around
I tried to make it up to you, somehow
But my words were not good enough, though sound

I meant the three small-huge words I told you
No, I'm not speaking of the ones you dread
(Though, for the record, I did mean those too)
But, "I don't know"; that statement I once said

I know you won't remember its meaning
But, to me, sharing it meant everything

Daydreaming

Don't tell me not to live in the past

The regrets in my mind will ever last

Yes, in theory it's good advice

But if you think it's so simple you better think twice

Don't tell me not to ask 'what if'

Without these dreams I might as well be stiff

I can't confine myself to the present

Considering today just isn't pleasant

Thinking of a better future

Or how I'd redo it all

Consumes my mind

But for a time, till I get that wake-up call

Remembrance

It was a warm day; especially sunny for an April morning, but sadness hung low in the air. Alice was running through the meadow, her long golden locks brushing past the overgrown wildflowers. As much as he tried, James, her father, just couldn't keep up. He shouted after her but it was no use, there was no stopping her.

James looked weary and distressed simultaneously. He stopped for a moment and waited for it.

Alice screamed, just as he expected, and he started walking again, slower this time. He was just as scared as she was.

Just as the ruins came into James' line of vision, Alice ran back up the path towards him and into his arms, burying her head in his arms. He stood still again, looking unsure before turning around to walk back the way he came.

Alice's head jolted up at his movement and she screamed again but this time it was in anger and was directed towards her father.

"You promised!" she wailed.

"This is a bad idea, cupcake. Look how upset we both are already."

"But you haven't given mom our message yet. She won't know we came."

James took in a deep breath as he fought back the dampness collecting behind his glasses; turning again, he continued down the path once more. Alice wriggled out of his arms and led him by the hand to the ruins at the foot of the hill.

The stonework of what was once an idyllic little cottage was scattered all over the ground, still dusted with heavy soot like the last time James saw it, but now with moss growing in various places too.

He couldn't hold back the tears anymore. Kneeling down, James tried to cover his face, so as not to show Alice *quite* how upset he was.

In a broken voice he warned her to be careful and not to touch anything.

After wandering around for a little while, Alice returned to her father's side and asked him to tell her the story again.

Taking a deep breath, James began.

"When you were a little baby, your mom and I lived here." He stood up and took a few steps back, to perch on a nearby wall that originally marked the boundary between garden and meadow. Alice climbed up to sit in his lap.

"She was beautiful, wasn't she? You said that. You said she was beautiful, before."

“Your mother was very beautiful. A lot like you” a sad smile eased across his face at the thought. “She loved it here; living so close to nature; would pick a fresh flower for her hair every day. Had golden hair the same as you, blue eyes too. One day she went out to check on all the animal pens, down by the river, while I read to you at home. She was gone a long time and, as night fell there was still no sign.
A storm was brewing. I was getting worried and I...”

Alice placed her little hand on top her father’s; silently reassuring him.

“I didn’t know what to do. The police came out to evacuate us. He said the storm was going to be really big and I wanted to go and look for your mother but I couldn’t leave you alone in the house and I wasn’t going to give you to the officer because the howling wind had already spooked you. So I took you to the school they’d opened to temporarily house the evacuees. I thought your mom might be there already but when I didn’t see her, I made the police promise they’d search for her and pass on the news that we were safe. They did search, for a while, but soon it was too dark and the storm had fully kicked in."

James' speech broke off again.

"Tell me about what they found her with. I like that bit."
"When they found her she was back at the cottage, cradling the huge soft toy we'd bought you for your christening."
"She missed us, huh?"
"She loved us more than anything."

"Do you think she knew the lightening would hit the cottage before it did? Do you think she was scared?" asked Alice, sounding so grown up. "Where do you think she was, all the time she was gone?"

James thought in silence for a bit. It looked as if he was considering making something up, or rose-tinting the truth.

In the end he said, “I really don’t know. I’ve asked myself hundreds of times...”

“Me too” came Alice’s small voice in return. It seemed distant somehow.

“I’m sorry. I shouldn’t have brought you here. I shouldn’t tell you these things.”

“No. I need to know. And I demanded to come, remember?”

“I remember.”

“Good. Now give me the card we made, so I can put it on mommy’s grave.”

James smiled “You’re gonna be a real warrior someday.”

“I don’t know what you mean” said Alice, “but I think it’s a good thing.”

“It is. No one will ever mess with *‘Alice the strong.’*”

“Was mommy strong?”

“Yes. Just like you.”

Time

Past, Present and Future

I have issues with each of you

No matter how hard I've tried, in the past, I just can't quite let

go of you,

Past

No, the irony's not lost on me

How all this time has

Passed

Just gone

And today's present used to be the future, yesterday

And so on

Present, aren't you supposed to be aptly titled?

Isn't each passing moment a gift?

If indeed it is, then what of the moments past?

Are moments gifts only while they are still moments?

Or do they take on the form of a greater gift, when combined
in the packaging of years and months, days and weeks?

And, Oh, dear future! Why must you tease us?
The less said about your wayward ways, the better!

Frustrating how time is
Complex yet simplified into just three categories
I fear it is not as linear as we first thought
With its wibbles and wobbles

I hope to understand fully, one day, the concept of time
And it's passing
Maybe then I'll be content
Doubt it'll happen in this life, though

I could go on to wonder, if time isn't linear, about the
possibility of lives overlapping but alas,

It’s far too late for that.

Sleep must come now; after all, it is what is generally

considered to be “bedtime”

(And oh what a hideous sub-concept that is!)

Short and Sour

You worry me sometimes,

When you're upset and I don't know why,

Maybe I could help…

Why won't you let me try?

Born of Death

At the end of her first week at university studying philosophy, Willow Wilson was called into her chief lecture's office.

"Willow"

"Yes, sir?"

The lecturer smiled a little. Most people didn't call him sir.

"Please, call me Mike. Do you know why you're here?"

"Here, sir? In this office, in this body, in this life? You'll have to be a little more specific."

Mike's smile widened.

"Very good, miss Wilson" said the lecturer, now feeling the need to address Willow as formally as she did him. "It's good to know *someone* was paying attention to my opening lecture."

Willow nodded but remained silent.

"Miss Wilson, as I'm sure you are aware, the faculty set an assignment before term commenced that was due to be handed in at the end of the first lecture."

Willow's soft brown eyes widened.

"I did the essay. Did you not get it?"

"Oh, we got it."

Relaxing a little, Willow replaced the look of worry on her face with one of confusion but once more remained silent.

"When we set the assignment each year we do it to prepare the students for hard work. Now, don't quote me on this but, we don't expect first assignments to be very good. After all, the students who write them have yet to be trained in the art of thinking, let alone writing."

Willow was offended at the man's pretentiousness and it was obvious from the look on her face but Mike ignored it.

"Perhaps you should rethink university, Willow" – all formality had been dropped again.

"What?!" said she, in loud indignation.

"I've spoke with my colleagues and it would appear we all agree. You have major issues. Need a great deal of therapy, or something."

"Just what issues do I have that make you think I shouldn't be a student?"

"Your essay was exquisitely written. You spoke so deeply about death, referring to it as if it were a parent in many paragraphs of your essay. So, either you stole the essay from someone else or your mind is little *too* dark and twisted for this place."

"How dare you?!"

It was now Mike's turn to be silent.

"Where do you get off being so judgemental? Death is something very real to me, very tangible. If I write about it exquisitely, as you say, then why is that a problem?"

"That's the kind of thing we can't have you coming out with."

"Dr Herd, with all due respect, I'd like to speak now without being cut off. You are not better than me and your opinion is not more important. I refuse to let you away with hurling around such accusations without giving me a chance to say my piece.

You talk of me leaving university – something that would no doubt affect the rest of my life – as if it is of so little consequence.

“When I was born my name wasn’t Willow Wilson, sir. My father changed it when I was about three. Damn near the only good thing he ever did for me.”

Mike looked unimpressed at the explanation so far but what Willow said next really made him sit up and take notice.

“My real name, my birth name, is Kendra Woodhouse.”

“Kendra Woodhouse? *THE* Kendra Woodhouse? The miracle baby, born of a corpse?! From all the newspapers, way back when?”

“The very same.”

“Wow” said Mike, seeming genuinely shocked.

“I had a grave where I should have had a mother. I had a broken man dependent on alcohol, instead of a father. At many times I felt much closer to death than I ever did my biological relations. So, you see, I wrote what I knew. I wrote well because I knew well; a little too well, I admit.

I do not have issues sir, I just have a crap past and that is something you have no right to hold against me. I, nor anyone else for that matter, do not need to be taught how to think, especially not from the likes of you; someone who doesn’t even listen to his own preaching about asking questions and never assuming.

I'll pack up my things and leave tonight."

"That won't be necessary. I understand now."

"You understand nothing. You have no intention of even apologising for the way you've handled this."

"If I apologise would it make you willing to let me interview you? Let me write a paper about your experience of coffin birth?"

Willow sighed. "Just another greedy little man, wanting to cash in on other people's misery. I pity you. Good day - sir!"

Away with the Fairies

There once was a girl, we all knew

Infamous for being odd, it is true

With a wonky haircut and a crooked smile to boot

She was an odd lookin' being; the word "harmless" tattooed on her foot

If you knew how much she enjoyed it you'd chose craziness too

Midnight Musings

Why can people say, 'this is my favourite time of day' and it be 'normal'?
Yet not state, 'this is my favourite time of night'?
Without acquiring queer looks
And assumptions that one is talking only of the moonlit hours?

Is the night not the same length as the day?
On average, I mean, of course -
Seasonal variation aside.

WHY DO people say day when they mean a period that includes both day and night?

Oh how such things frustrate me!
I know that it is, of little consequence
In the grand scheme of things
I just prefer the night.
Night should be given its dues.

Now That We're Done

I do care, but I don't mind

You're not gonna get me this time

I'm beyond worrying about you every second, of every day

So I'm not gonna let you get to me

Because I've seen you're tricks

And I'm sick of your games

I'm not doing this again

You called it love

But I see now

You don't know what that means

You made a fool out of me

So bully for you

What are you gonna do?

I'm moving on and where are you?

Yes

I do feel guilty for being so harsh

But you left very little choice

I do care, but I don’t mind

After everything,

I’ve stopped thinking about it all so much

I’m letting go

But, for the record,

I will always still care

Because that’s who I am

And what I do

It actually has very little to do with you

Let go

Move on

God knows I had to

Real Love

Roaring waves of fire

Soft and gentle, earnest desire

An inner conflict

Keeping control to not get hurt

Heart ignoring mind

Letting go 'cause it's worth it.

A bittersweet joy

The Room at the End of the Hall

For all intents and purposes, the room at the end of the hall does not exist.

It can only be found by people who, not only are not looking for it, but are not even thinking about it (which is a rare occurrence due to the great deal of rumour surrounding the place). It is hard to go a couple of days without one of the gossips who work in the kitchens below dreaming up a new piece of folklore about the room. It is on no floor plan that I've ever seen, and I was almost certain it was nothing but a well crafted myth. That was until I stumbled through the door myself, just last night while on my way to bed.

What is it exactly? What is in there? No one really knows and there is no use asking me, for it is mainly overtired workers that walk in and the room has such a disorientating feel to it that all memories fade as soon as you leave, making the person doubt their own sanity within minutes of returning to the hallway. That's the way it was for me too.

Some say the door is a gateway to a parallel universe and, having thought on it for quite some time myself, I must say that I now have more questions than answers and *any* theory – no matter how farfetched – now seems possible.

One thing I do know, however, is that the old gamekeeper, Mr Travers, claims to know all about it and maintains every time he's asked that there's no mystery at all. He doesn't understand what all the fuss is about – says it's just a normal room, with a normal door and "of course anyone can go in".

I've always thought he was crazy, with his clothes and manners like something from a hundred year ago.

Eccentric, that's the word for him.

It's strange though, now I come to think of it, that he's even still around considering we sold all the land last year. Martha says he's not even on the payroll.

Note to Self

At times you'll want to give up
– WORK HARDER DESPITE IT

You'll want to give in
– WALK AWAY FROM TEMPTATION

You'll want to run away
– STAND FIRM IN THE FACE OF FEAR

You'll want to hide way
– BE BOLD ANYWAY

You'll want to end it
– KEEP LIVING ANWAY

You'll be able to get away with half hearted effort
– GIVE IT YOUR ALL

You'll be given a job you don't feel qualified for
– DO THE BEST DAMN JOB YOU KNOW HOW TO DO

You'll have unpleasant tasks and want to make excuses
– BE HONEST ABOUT YOUR APREHENSIONS AND GET OVER THEM

You'll be hungry, tired, injured and cold
– DO NOT GIVE UP

You'll make mistakes and, at times, make a hypocrite of yourself
– REPENT AND DO BETTER!

It may be harsh but, in the end, you'll have a strength no one can shift.
All glory to God!

Triumph

I may not have made it yet,

But I know now what's the key

Yes, everyone always said it

But I never quite understood

How people could take lumps of poison

And use them for a fire, like wood

It took me a while

Much longer than most

But I've turned their put downs into fuel

The fire in my gut's now burning

I'm not gonna be their fool

The people were right

The ones that said,

"You have to prove them wrong"

But that never was my way of thinking

Because, how did I know –

The dream crushers weren't right all along?

I took their poison words on board
And they kept my flame damped down
Damn near snuffed it out at times
But they never quite got that far

Oh, yet more irony!
That the ones proclaiming defeat,
Upon everyone else but them, should fail
Their own task of crushing spirits, they did not meet

I beat them
And although they will never say so
I proved it to each last one of them
That I'll be the last to go

I may not have made it yet,
But I know now what's the key
I've disregarded all their poison

And stocked up on positivity

Yes, I know how cliché it sounds

But I'll say it 'cause it's true

My triumph wasn't in earning big

But in taking hold of this, new attitude

It's one that will get me far

And you too, if you want

Go and spite the naysayers, because

"You have to prove them wrong"

Fin.